123 SESAME STREET®

Goodnight Treasury

18 Classic Stories

Dover Publications, Inc.
Mineola, New York

Copyright

Bibliographical Note

Sesame Street Goodnight Treasury—18 Classic Stories, is a new compilation, first published by Dover Publications, Inc., in 2011, containing the following books: *Big Bird's New Nest and Other Goodnight Stories*, first published by Golden Books Publishing Company, Inc., New York, in cooperation with Children's Television Workshop in 1989; *Ernie and His Merry Monsters and Other Goodnight Stories*, first published by Golden Books Publishing Company, Inc., New York, in cooperation with Children's Television Workshop in 1992; *What's in Oscar's Trash Can and Other Goodnight Stories,* first published by Western Publishing Company, Inc., Racine, Wisconsin, in 1991; *Cookie Soup and Other Goodnight Stories,* first published by Golden Books Publishing Company, Inc., New York, in cooperation with Children's Television Workshop in 1990; *Herry's New Shoes and Other Goodnight Stories,* first published by Golden Books Publishing Company, Inc., New York, in cooperation with Children's Television Workshop in 1989; and *When Oscar Was a Little Grouch and Other Goodnight Stories*, first published by Golden Books Publishing Company, Inc., New York, in cooperation with Children's Television Workshop in 1989.

International Standard Book Number

ISBN-13: 978-0-486-33035-8
ISBN-10: 0-486-33035-4

Manufactured in the United States by Courier Corporation
33035401
www.doverpublications.com

CONTENTS

BIG BIRD'S NEW NEST
Oscar's Grouchy Vacation . . . 3
Big Bird's New Nest . . . 13
Grover, Go to Sleep! . . . 17

ERNIE AND HIS MERRY MONSTERS
Ernie and His Merry Monsters . . . 23
The Big Bad Grouch . . . 33
Cookie Crumbs . . . 37

WHAT'S IN OSCAR'S TRASH CAN?
What's in Oscar's Trash Can? . . . 43
Bert's Birthday . . . 51
The End of the Day . . . 58

COOKIE SOUP
Big Bird and the Lost Bear . . . 62
Cookie Soup . . . 70
Never Ask a Honker to Spend the Night . . . 78

HERRY'S NEW SHOES
Herry's New Shoes . . . 83
One Wet Monster . . . 89
Is it Time for Bed Yet? . . . 97

WHEN OSCAR WAS A LITTLE GROUCH
When Oscar Was a Little Grouch . . . 103
Tina Twiddlebug's Big Adventure . . . 109
Goodnight, Bert! . . . 115

Big Bird's New Nest
and Other Goodnight Stories

By Justine Korman
Illustrated by Tom Cooke

OSCAR'S GROUCHY VACATION

"Thank you for helping me carry my groceries," Maria told Big Bird.

"You're welcome," said Big Bird. "I like helping my friends."

"So do I," said Maria. "Please let me know if there is anything I can do for you."

"Yucch!" Oscar the Grouch grumbled in his trash can. "All this niceness is making me sick!" He banged the lid of his can, but even that dreadful din didn't cheer him up.

"I need a vacation," he said with a sigh.

So Oscar rummaged around in his can until he found a tattered flyer from Grouch Tours, Inc. It showed pictures of vacations guaranteed to satisfy even the grouchiest grouch. Oscar couldn't decide between "Town Dumps of New England" and "Trash Cans of the Rich and Famous." Then he noticed that the New England tour left in less than an hour.

"That's the tour for me," Oscar said. "I'm getting away from this sweetness now."

Oscar packed his tattered old suitcases and told the mail carrier to save all his junk mail. Then he hurried to the bus station.

"Have a nice day," the ticket-seller told Oscar.

"I hope not," grumbled the grouch. And he was so busy grouching that he forgot to find out where to wait for his bus.

Just then an announcement came over the loudspeaker: "Fall Foliage and Fun Tour departs in one minute. Grouch Tour bus leaving now!"

So Oscar ran to the nearest platform.

As soon as the bus started moving, Oscar noticed that all the other passengers were neat and cheerful. When he asked where they were going, he was told, "This is the Fall Foliage and Fun Tour."

"Oh, no! Beautiful, changing, colorful leaves? I'm on the wrong bus! Let me off!" yelled Oscar.

But the driver said, "I'm sorry, sir. The next town isn't for fifty miles."

A nice person on the bus tried to comfort Oscar.

"You'll have a fun time on this tour," he told him. "Look at that bright orange patch on the horizon! The leaves are so lovely at this time of year."

Oscar fell back in his seat, grumbling, "I might as well have stayed on Sesame Street."

The bus stopped at the side of the road, and all the passengers got off to look at the dazzling autumn leaves.

"Look at that bright yellow tree!" said a cheerful child.

"I like the red ones," another child chimed in.

Oscar didn't like the bright colors. But he did enjoy the way the leaves blew everywhere, sticking to sweaters and getting tangled in fur and piling up in messy heaps.

8

The next stop was the beach. Oscar ignored the glittering ocean waves and the white sand. Instead, he looked for litter and old soda bottles in the dunes.

He watched the seagulls break open mussels on the rocks, scattering shells everywhere. And he liked the seaweed the waves left behind.

When the tour stopped at a farm stand, Oscar couldn't find anything at all to please a grouch. There were neat pyramids of fresh apples and pears, carefully arranged jugs of apple juice, and shelves of homemade jams, jellies, and pies. It was enough to make a grouch scream!

Oscar took a deep breath. Suddenly he smelled something that made his grouchy heart leap with glee.

It was the smoky smell of burning trash. Oscar followed the smell to the town dump. There he saw a group of grouches eagerly sifting and searching through heaps of abandoned bicycles, broken toasters, and beat-up egg beaters. They were looking for grouchy souvenirs.

Nearby, he saw a rusty bus with a sign that said "Grouch Tours" on the front and "Have a Grouchy Day" on the side.

"It's my group!" Oscar exclaimed, and he ran toward the other grouches. They growled glum greetings and welcomed Oscar into the Grouch Tour group.

Oscar ran from heap to heap, up to his fuzzy elbows in New England trash. Soon his fur was covered in soot.

"Now, this is my kind of vacation!" Oscar said, sighing. "Maybe tomorrow will be even worse!"

BIG BIRD'S NEW NEST

"Thanks for helping me move, Snuffy," Big Bird told his friend Mr. Snuffleupagus.

"You're welcome," replied Snuffy. "I wish I could stay and help you settle in, but we're planning a surprise party for my sister, Alice, and I need to hurry home."

Big Bird waved good-bye to Mr. Snuffleupagus and then looked around at his new home. It was full of bags, boxes, and suitcases.

"Well, I'd better start unpacking!" Big Bird said out loud.

So Big Bird moved his giant bed of twigs into a cozy corner.

"There! Now the morning sun will peep over the fence and say, 'Good morning, Big Bird. It's time to wake up.'"

Big Bird looked around. "But my new home doesn't feel like a home yet," he said.

13

"I know!" said Big Bird. "My new home looks like a home, but it doesn't sound like a home."

So Big Bird searched through a big box marked "records" and found his favorite, "Chirp Around the Clock." He put it on the record player and chirped and hummed along.

While Big Bird listened to the music he unpacked more boxes and bags. He moved his night table next to his bed. He found his reading lamp and put that on his night table. He tucked away his writing notebooks and a can of sharpened crayons on a little shelf over the bed.

Big Bird felt better. But somehow his new place still was not home.

So Big Bird searched through a box marked "kitchen." He found his biggest bowl, a spoon, and a measuring cup. Then he mixed a batch of his special chocolate-chip cookies. Soon his new home was filled with the warm, sweet aroma of baking cookies.

"Now my new home smells like home," he said. When the cookies were ready, Big Bird pulled them out of the oven. He bit into a warm cookie. "Now it tastes like home, but there is still something missing."

Just then a pair of round, googly eyes peeped over the fence.
"Me come in?" asked a hungry blue monster.

"Please do," said Big Bird. "Welcome to my new home.
Would you like some cookies?"

"Don't mind if I do," said Cookie Monster, and he gobbled
up all the cookies.

Big Bird smiled. "That's what my new home needed! A visit
from a friend. Now this place is home!"

GROVER, GO TO SLEEP!

Grover's mother looked at the clock and put down her book.
"It is time to go to bed, dear," she told Grover.
Grover was whirling around in his Super Grover cape and
helmet, making the world safe for furry monsters.
"Do I have to?" he asked.
Grover's mother nodded. "Yes, you do."

Grover sighed. He took off his cape and helmet. He washed his furry blue face, brushed his teeth, and put on his flannel pajamas. But he still did not want to go to bed.

"May I please have a cup of hot cocoa?" Grover asked.

So his mommy brought him a cup of cocoa.

"Oh, my goodness!" said Grover. "You forgot the marshmallows."

So Grover's mommy went back to the kitchen and brought two marshmallows.

"Will you read me a bedtime story?" he asked.

So Grover's mommy read him a story about a prince, a princess, and a grouchy old wizard.

When it was finished, she asked, "Now will you go to sleep, please?"

"You forgot something, Mommy. You forgot to say that the prince and princess lived happily ever after."

So Grover's mommy said, "The prince and princess lived happily ever after.

"Is that better?" asked Grover's mommy.

"Yes, but you still forgot something. You forgot to say, The End."

"The End," said Grover's mommy. She smiled and kissed his forehead.

"Now go to sleep, Grover," she said.

"Okay, Mommy, but I have just one more thing to ask you. Would you sing me a lullaby?" Grover asked.

So Grover's mommy sat in her chair and rocked back and forth and sang "Rockabye Monster." She sang all the verses. She sang all the "la-la-la-las." She sang the squirrels and chipmunks on the windowsill to sleep. She sang the little bird in the tree to sleep. And, finally, she sang Grover to sleep, too.

SESAME STREET

Ernie and His Merry Monsters

and Other Goodnight Stories

By Michaela Muntean
Illustrated by Tom Leigh

ERNIE AND
HIS MERRY MONSTERS

"That Robin Hood was a great guy," Ernie said to himself. "He and his merry men must have had a wonderful time living in Sherwood Forest and doing good deeds."

Ernie leaned back against a tree trunk. "Those were the days," he thought. "Sometimes I think we could use a hero like Robin Hood on Sesame Street."

Ernie closed his storybook and then he closed his eyes. Soon he was asleep, dreaming dreams of Robin Hood.

"Help! Someone help me, please," cried a little boy.

Luckily Robin Hood was nearby and heard the boy's cry. "What's the matter?" asked Robin Hood.

"My kitten, Fluffy, is in this tree, and he can't get down," said the boy.

"Don't worry," said Robin Hood. "I will blow my horn, and soon you'll have Fluffy back safe and sound."

The little boy stared at the figure dressed in green. "I've already tried calling and whistling," he said. "I don't think blowing a horn is going to help."

"Just wait and see," said Robin Hood, and he blew three loud blasts on his horn. A few moments later three monsters came running down the street.

"This is my band of merry monsters," Robin Hood explained to the boy. "Meet Friar Tuck, Little John, and Will Scarlet."

"Wow!" said the boy. "That must mean *you* are Robin Hood."

"At your service," Robin Hood said with a bow. "We travel far and wide, doing good deeds and other heroic stuff. But now to the job at hand! Give me a boost, merry monsters, and I will rescue Fluffy."

The boy watched as Robin Hood and his merry monsters got
Fluffy down from the tree. Soon the kitten was snuggled safely
in the boy's arms.

"Thank you," said the little boy. "You were so brave!"

"Bravery is our business," Robin Hood answered. Then he
and his merry monsters set off down Sesame Street in search
of other good deeds that needed doing.

They hadn't gone far when they noticed a lady pacing nervously up and down the sidewalk. She looked very worried.

"May we help you?" asked Robin Hood.

"I dropped my ring and it rolled down there," said the lady, pointing to a grate in the street. "I'm afraid I'll never get it back," she added sadly.

Robin Hood peered through the metal bars of the grate. Sure enough, deep in the hole below the grate was the lady's ring.

"My merry monsters and I will help you," Robin Hood said to the lady. Then he whispered something to Will Scarlet, and Will ran off. He returned a few minutes later carrying a fishing pole.

Robin Hood tied a small magnet to the end of the fishing line.
Then he lowered it through the grate. It was not long before he
was reeling in the line, the magnet, *and* the ring.

"Oh, thank you," said the lady when Robin Hood handed her
the ring. "That was so clever of you!"

"Being clever is part of our job," said Robin Hood as he and
his merry monsters took a deep bow.

Someone was crying. At first Ernie thought it was part of his
dream, but when he opened his eyes, he knew it wasn't. A little
girl really *was* crying, and Herry, Elmo, and Cookie Monster
were telling her not to worry.

"What's wrong?" Ernie asked.

"I've lost my puppy," said the little girl.

"And we're going to help look for him," said Herry.

Ernie did what he thought Robin Hood would do. "Let's organize a search party," he said.

It took a lot of searching, but at last they spotted the puppy, who had fallen asleep beneath some bushes.

"Thank you for helping me," said the little girl.

"Being helpful is our business," Ernie said.

No one knew what he meant, but that didn't matter. Ernie knew. He knew there were times when a hero like Robin Hood was just what Sesame Street needed.

THE BIG BAD GROUCH

Oscar took a deep breath and blew as hard as he could. He took another breath, and then another, huffing and puffing over and over again.

Big Bird was on his way home, but he stopped to watch. He couldn't figure out what Oscar was doing, so he asked him.

"Can't you see I'm practicing?" said Oscar.

"Practicing what?" Big Bird asked.

"The Grouch Theater is putting on *The Big Bad Wolf,* and I'm going to try out for the leading role," Oscar explained. "I have to practice huffing and puffing and blowing down houses."

Big Bird scratched his head. "I thought that story was called *The Three Little Pigs,*" he said.

"Listen up, birdbrain," said Oscar. "I told you this is a grouch production."
"But you need the three pigs or you don't have a story," said Big Bird.
"Yeah, I know," Oscar admitted. "It's always a problem when we put on a play at the Grouch Theater. Every grouch wants the rottenest part—like the witch or the giant. This time everyone wants to play the wolf. No respectable grouch wants to play one of those silly pigs who built his house out of sticks or straw."

"The third little pig wasn't silly," said Big Bird. "He built his house out of bricks."

"That's true," said Oscar, "but the part of the wolf is the only part for me. Look, I've already made a poster." He held up a sheet of paper with his picture on it. Under the picture it read:

STARRING
OScaR THe GRouCH
AS
THE BiG BAD WOLF

"You've got to admit I make a wonderful wolf," he said.

"You were born for the part," Big Bird agreed. He was about to remind Oscar that the pigs catch the wolf at the end of the story when Oscar said, "You'd better beat it, feather face. I've got to get back to blowing practice. I don't want to *blow* my chances for the part. Heh-heh-heh. Get it?"

"I get it," said Big Bird. "And I hope you get the part, Oscar. A grouch like you deserves it!"

COOKIE CRUMBS

Elmo was on his way to do an errand for his mother. He had to buy some milk at Hooper's Store.

Before he left home, his mother had given him three oatmeal cookies. Elmo ate one of them right away and put the others in his pocket.

As he walked toward the store, Elmo thought about the story his mother had read him the night before. It was called *Hansel and Gretel.* Elmo thought it was clever of Hansel to leave a trail of breadcrumbs so he could find his way home.

Elmo felt for the cookies in his pocket, and that gave him an idea. "I know," he said. "I will pretend I am Hansel and leave a trail of cookie crumbs. Then I'll follow them back home!"

Elmo broke off bits of the cookies and dropped them on the sidewalk. He left a cookie trail to Hooper's Store.

After he bought the milk, he looked for the trail he had left, but there wasn't one cookie crumb to be found.

When Elmo got home, he told his mother how he had pretended he was Hansel and had left a trail of cookie crumbs. "But the birds must have eaten them," he said.

From the window came a tweet, tweet sound. Elmo looked up to see Cookie Monster. He was flapping his arms and making sounds like a bird. Both Elmo and his mother laughed.

"It's lucky for me that I know my way home!" said Elmo.

"And it's lucky I have two more cookies," said Elmo's mother. "One for my little red monster—and one for this big blue 'bird'!"

What's in Oscar's Trash Can?
and Other Goodnight Stories

By Michaela Muntean
Illustrated by Tom Cooke

WHAT'S IN OSCAR'S TRASH CAN?

"Whew! Is it ever hot!" said Elmo.

"Let's go get an ice-cream cone," said Ernie. "Maybe that will help us cool off." Elmo thought that was a great idea, so they headed toward Hooper's Store.

As they passed Oscar's can they noticed a sign.

"'GROUCH REUNION,'" Ernie read.

"What a day for a reunion!" said Elmo. "I'll bet those grouches are even grouchier than usual on a hot day like this."

Just then they heard the rattle of the trash-can lid, and up popped Oscar.

"Brrr," he said. "The water in that swimming pool is chilly. I need to warm up a bit."

"Pool?" asked Elmo. "What pool?"

"*My* pool, of course," said Oscar. "Whose swimming pool do you think I'm talking about?"

"Gee, Oscar," said Ernie, "I never even knew you *had* a swimming pool."

"We grouches are full of surprises," Oscar said, chuckling. "Heh-heh. You should see Uncle Oswaldo and Filthomena! They had a big water fight, and both of them are soaked! Then Fluffy the elephant got in the act and sprayed Grundgetta with his trunk. It was great!"

"An elephant?" cried Elmo. "You mean an *elephant* lives down there with you?" "Sure," Oscar said with a shrug.

"What else is in your can, Oscar?" asked Ernie.

"Do you mean besides the ice-skating rink?" Oscar asked.

"Ice-skating rink?" Elmo cried.

"Yep." Oscar nodded. "And that reminds me. Slimey's been practicing making figure eights all week. He's going to put on a show, and I don't want to miss it! After that we're going to have a picnic. I'm serving stinkweed coleslaw, burnt potato chips, and hot dogs smothered with sardines."

"Yucch," said Elmo, but Ernie quickly said, "Gee, Oscar, that sounds pretty good, especially if we could go swimming first. Say, would you mind if we came to your reunion?"

"Mind? Of course I'd mind!" Oscar cried. "We're having a *grouch* reunion, and as far as I know, neither one of you is a grouch."

"We *could* be," said Elmo.

Oscar frowned and pulled out a mirror. He held it up to
Elmo and said, "Take a look and tell me what you see."
Elmo looked at his reflection in the mirror. "I see one cute
little red monster," he said.
Oscar held up the mirror for Ernie. "Do you see a grumpy face
with thick, scowly eyebrows?"
"No," Ernie admitted.
"Well, that proves it," Oscar said. "Neither one of you is a real grouch."

Then from the depths of the trash can they heard angry voices shouting and arguing.

"Heh-heh," laughed Oscar. "They're fighting over who gets to bowl first. There's nothing like a grouch reunion to bring out the worst in everyone! I certainly don't want to miss a good argument. So long, and have a really hot, rotten day!"

And with a crash of the trash can lid, he was gone.

Elmo scratched his head and looked at Ernie. "Do you really think that Oscar has a bowling alley in his can?" he asked.

Slowly Ernie lifted up the edge of the lid and peeked inside the trash can. "I can't see anything," he said with a shrug. "Let's go get that ice-cream cone."

As they walked away they heard loud rumbling. They stopped to look at each other.

"Doesn't that *sound* like bowling, Ernie?" asked Elmo.

"Nah," said Ernie. "It *couldn't* be. Could it?"

BERT'S BIRTHDAY

The first thing Bert saw when he opened his eyes was Ernie staring at him.

"Gee, Bert, it's about time you woke up!" Ernie said. "Let me be the first to wish you a happy birthday, old buddy!"

Bert sat up in bed and looked at the clock. "But, Ernie," he groaned, "of course you're the first! It's six o'clock in the morning!"

"I thought you'd want to get an early start on celebrating," Ernie said. "Just wait until you hear what I've planned for today."

"I can hardly wait," Bert grumbled as he climbed out of bed and put on his bathrobe and slippers.

"I'll be waiting in the kitchen for you," Ernie said as Bert shuffled off toward the bathroom.

While Bert brushed his teeth and got dressed, Ernie set the table. He was all ready when Bert walked into the kitchen.

"Notice anything special about what we're having for breakfast?" Ernie asked.

Bert looked at the bowl of blueberries, the glass of buttermilk, and the slices of banana bread. But before he could answer, Ernie said, "Do you get it, Bert? Everything starts with the letter *B*! That's because today is your birthday, Bert, and both *birthday* and *Bert* start with the letter *B*. Did you ever think about that, Bert?"

"Not really, Ernie," Bert answered.

"That's why you've got me for a friend, old buddy," Ernie said. "I'm here to think of these things for you. We're going to have a whole *day* filled with the letter *B*!"

Bert smiled and buttered a piece of banana bread. "You know, Ernie, now that I'm awake, I'm beginning to think it's a good idea. What are we going to do?"

"Gee, Bert, I'm glad you asked, because we have to get going right now. Come on!" Ernie cried, and he led the way down the stairs to Sesame Street. They reached the bus stop just as a big blue bus pulled up.

"Where are we going?" Bert asked when they had found seats.

Ernie smiled. "It's a surprise," he said.

After a while Ernie said, "We get off at the next stop."

53

When they got off the bus, Bert said, "Ernie, this is my favorite beach!"

"I know, Bert," said Ernie. "Remember, this is B-day, and *beach* starts with the letter *B*. And look, I remembered to bring your bathing suit, a beach ball, our toy boats, and a badminton set."

All morning Ernie and Bert played on the beach. When it was time for lunch, Ernie opened a big basket. "I brought baloney sandwiches, two bottles of Burpee soda, a three-bean salad, and brownies."

"Why, everything starts with the letter *B*," Bert said.

"Now you're getting the idea," Ernie said.

After lunch Bert said, "This has been a great day, Ernie. Thanks."

"It's not over yet," said Ernie. "In fact, this is just the beginning. Come on, we've got to get back home."

When the bus stopped at 123 Sesame Street, Ernie hurried up the stairs, and Bert followed.

"Ta-da!" Ernie cried as he opened the door. There stood all of their friends, singing "Happy birthday, Bert." Balloons hung from the ceiling, and boxes were piled on the table.

All of Bert's presents started with the letter *B*, too. Grover gave him a bird book. Big Bird had baked him a batch of birdseed cookies. The Count gave him a box filled with bottle caps. Elmo gave him a brick with the letter *B* painted on it. "It's a paperweight," Elmo explained.

That night, when everyone had gone home, Bert said, "Thank you, Ernie. That was the best birthday I've ever had."

"Really, Bert?"

"You *bet*," said Bert. "It was *beautiful*, *brilliant*, and a real *blast*."

THE END OF THE DAY
By Ernie

Sometimes, at the end of the day, I like to sit quietly on the front stoop. My shadow stretches out in front of me, but because of the steps, it has crinkles in it like the folds in an accordion.

Soon the streetlights come on, and I can see tiny bugs flying around them. I wonder if the bugs were there all the time, and I couldn't see them because there weren't any lights. Or did they fly over when the lights came on? There's time to think about these things when you sit on the stoop at the end of the day.

I hear mothers and fathers calling to their children to stop playing and come inside.

"El-mo," calls Elmo's mother, and her voice trails off like a train whistle.

"Nick!" calls Nick's father, and his voice is quick and sharp, like a dog's bark.

"Mar-eee-anne," calls another mother, and it sounds like she is singing a song. I hope Mary Anne doesn't go in right away so I can hear her mother call her again.

Another thing I hear is Prairie Dawn practicing the piano. On Mondays, when she is learning a new song, she plays slowly and makes a lot of mistakes. But by Friday she can play the song all the way through without any mistakes at all.

I see Luis turn out the lights in the Fix-It Shop. He turns over the OPEN sign so that now it says CLOSED. He locks the door. I wonder if he got everything fixed today. When he sees me sitting on the stoop, he waves, and I wave back.

As the sun creeps down behind the tall buildings up the street, I begin to feel cool. Now it's time for all the people on the other side of the world to have *their* turn with the sun. I put my head back and look straight up at the sky. When I see the first star of the evening, I close my eyes tight and make a wish. When I open my eyes again, there is another star. And another and then another. Soon there are so many stars that I can't count them.

Now it is dark and time to go inside. As I climb the steps I think about how nice it is to sit on the front stoop at the end of the day.

Cookie Soup

SESAME STREET

and Other Goodnight Stories

By Michaela Muntean
Illustrated by Joe Ewers

BIG BIRD AND THE LOST BEAR

One of Radar's button eyes hung loosely on a piece of thread. His coat was dirty and a bit of stuffing was coming out of one of his ears. "You don't look very well," Big Bird said as he carefully tucked his blanket around the little bear. "You had better stay in bed until I get back from play group." Big Bird patted Radar on the head. Then he waved good-bye and hurried to play group.

It was a busy morning. The class made sculptures out of clay. They colored pictures, played with blocks, and sang songs. It was Grover's turn for show-and-tell. He had brought a book about baby animals, and the teacher read it to the class. When she finished, she said, "Big Bird, next week it is your turn to bring something for show-and-tell."

"Oh, good!" said Big Bird. "I would like to bring my teddy bear, Radar." Then he remembered how Radar had looked earlier that morning. "Except he hasn't been feeling very well," said Big Bird sadly.

"Maybe he will be better next week," the teacher said.

"Yes," said Big Bird, "maybe he will." But for the rest of the morning, he couldn't help thinking about the little bear waiting for him at home.

When Big Bird got home from play group, he called out, "Radar, I'm back!"

But Radar wasn't there!

Big Bird looked under the blanket. "I'm *sure* I left him here," said Big Bird, scratching his head.

He looked in the nest again. He looked in his toy box and every drawer in his dresser. He looked on top of things and behind things and under things, but he couldn't find Radar.

Big Bird was worried. "Where could he have gone?" he said. He thought about Radar's button eye hanging on the piece of thread, and the stuffing coming out of his ear.

"That bear is in no shape to leave the nest. If I have to search every inch of Sesame Street, I will find him," said Big Bird.

On Sesame Street, Big Bird asked
everyone he met if they had seen Radar.
He asked the mail carrier, the garbage
collectors, and a truck driver. But every
answer was the same, and that answer
was no. No one had seen Radar.

Big Bird did not give up. He asked
Oscar, Ernie, and Bert. He asked at
Hooper's Store, and at Luis's Fix-It Shop.

He looked inside a telephone booth, on top of the mailbox, and under benches. He looked everywhere he thought a bear could be, but he did not find Radar.

Big Bird walked sadly down the street. As he passed the Wash and Dry Laundromat he glanced in the window. What he saw made him stop and hurry inside.

"Granny!" Big Bird cried.

"Big Bird!" Granny cried, giving him a hug. "I thought I'd surprise you and come for a visit. Radar didn't look too well, so I fixed him up and gave him a bath. I hope you weren't worried about him."

"I was," said Big Bird. "But I'm not anymore!"

Radar's button eye was sewn in place, his ear was mended, and he was soft and fluffy-clean.

"Oh, thank you, Granny!"

Big Bird gave Radar a big bird-hug. "I have a surprise for you, too, Radar! Next week you can come to play group with me."

COOKIE SOUP

When Ernie returned home from playing in the park, Cookie Monster was waiting for him.

"Congratulations," cried Cookie Monster. "Today is your lucky day. Me here to make dinner for you!"

Cookie Monster headed straight for the kitchen.

Ernie followed him. "But, Cookie," he said, "I don't think we have anything to make dinner *with*. We haven't been to the grocery store yet."

"Hmmm," said Cookie. "This is big problem, but luckily, me here to solve it for you! Do you have cookie?"

Ernie looked in the cookie jar. There was one oatmeal cookie left.

"COOKIE!" said Cookie Monster. "Just what we need to make cookie soup."

"*Cookie soup?*" asked Ernie.

"Yes," said Cookie. "It is delicious old Monster family recipe.
You will love it. First we need big pot."

Ernie found a big pot.

"Now we need water in pot," Cookie Monster said, and Ernie
filled the pot with water.

Soon the water in the pot was bubbling on the stove, and Cookie Monster
dropped the oatmeal cookie into it. In a few minutes, he tasted it.

"Mmmm," he said. "It is good, but it could use some salt and pepper."
Ernie handed Cookie Monster the salt and pepper shakers, and into the
simmering pot with the oatmeal cookie, Cookie Monster added

a pinch of salt

and a dash of pepper.

Cookie stirred and tasted the soup again. "We have to wait for flavor to cook in," he said. "While we wait, me look around."

He looked in the cupboard and found one onion and two potatoes. "ONION! POTATOES!" he cried. "They will make cookie soup even better!" And into the pot with

the oatmeal cookie,
a pinch of salt,
and a dash of pepper

he added:

one big red onion and
two round brown potatoes.

While the soup simmered on the stove Cookie Monster looked in the refrigerator. "You told me you had nothing to eat!" he cried. "But look at this! TOMATOES! CARROTS! CELERY!

"These will make cookie soup taste delicious," Cookie said. And into the pot with

the oatmeal cookie,
a pinch of salt,
a dash of pepper,
one big red onion, and
two round brown potatoes

he added:

three red ripe tomatoes,
four long orange carrots,
and five green stalks of celery.

Cookie Monster stirred the soup again. "What else have you got
in refrigerator?" he asked.

"There's some pickles and mayonnaise..."

"Pickles and mayonnaise not good in cookie soup. Anything
else?" "Well, there's some leftover roast beef" Ernie said.

"ROAST BEEF!" cried Cookie Monster. "Why you not tell me
this right away? Roast beef will make cookie soup best soup ever!"
And so into the pot with

> the oatmeal cookie,
> a pinch of salt,
> a dash of pepper,
> one big red onion,
> two round brown potatoes,
> three red ripe tomatoes,
> four long orange carrots, and
> five green stalks of celery

he added:

> six juicy slices of roast beef.

The soup began to smell good. Cookie Monster stirred it and tasted it. "It is ready! Now we eat *big* bowl of cookie soup."

Ernie tasted the soup and said, "You're right, Cookie. This cookie soup is delicious! I can't wait until Bert comes home. He'll never believe that we made this whole pot of soup with just one cookie!"

NEVER ASK A HONKER
TO SPEND THE NIGHT

"I, Grover, am here to give you some advice. It is very good advice, so listen carefully. Never, and I mean *never,* invite a Honker to spend the night at your house.

"Now, you may ask why. It is a good question, and I, Grover, will tell you the answer. It is because Honkers honk.

"From the minute they get to your house, they honk. They honk hello to your mommy. They honk while you help set the table for supper. Then they keep right on honking even while they eat!

"They honk while you help your mommy clear the table. They honk while you play checkers. They honk while your mommy makes popcorn for you, and then they keep on honking right through your favorite television program!

"When it is time to get ready for bed, they do not stop honking. They honk while they brush their teeth and comb their fur. They honk while they put on their pajamas. They honk as they climb into bed. They even honk while your mommy is reading you a goodnight story!

"But here is the worst part. Even after they are asleep, they do not stop honking. It sounds something like this: *honk-honk-shoooo, honk-honk-shoooo.*

"There is no way, and I mean *no way,* to block out that sound. You can try wrapping your pillow around your head. You can try wearing earplugs. You can even try sleeping out in the hallway, but nothing works.

"So that is why I, Grover, after saying good-bye to my Honker guests, am such a tired little monster this morning. Please remember this good advice, and never, ever, ever invite a Honker to spend the night at *your* house."

HERRY'S
NEW SHOES

AND OTHER GOODNIGHT STORIES

By Michaela Muntean
Illustrated by Carol Nicklaus

HERRY'S NEW SHOES

Herry Monster's furry big toe was poking out of one of his sneakers. His little toe was poking out of the other sneaker.

"Herry," said his mother, "I think it's time we bought you a new pair of shoes."

"But these shoes and I have been lots of places together. We are very good friends," he said.

"Those sneakers are getting too small for you," said Herry's mother. "Don't worry. You'll make friends with your new shoes, too."

So Herry and his mother walked to the shoe store. The salesman measured Herry's foot. "Hmmm," he said. "Size twelve. Pretty big for a monster your age." Then he went to the back room and brought out boxes and boxes of shoes.

Herry tried on blue sneakers, and red sneakers, and sneakers that laced all the way up to his ankles. At last he decided on a pair of white high tops with red stripes on the sides.

"They fit him perfectly," said the salesman.

"May I please wear them home?" Herry asked, and his mother said he could.

All the way back to Sesame Street, Herry kept looking down at his new shoes. They felt soft and cushiony on the inside, but stiff and squeaky when he walked.

"Well?" asked Herry's mother. "Do you think you and your new sneakers are going to be friends?"

"I don't know yet," said Herry. "I will have to show them around the neighborhood."

"All right," said Herry's mother, "but be sure you and your new shoes are home in time for dinner."

Herry headed toward the park. "Right now you are walking on cement," Herry said to his shoes. "It feels rough."

Then they reached the park. "Now you are walking on grass," Herry said. "It feels soft, and I'll bet it tickles you!

"Now I'll show you some of the things we will be doing together."

Herry jumped up and down. "That is jumping," Herry explained.

"And this is running," he said.

"Now I will show you around the neighborhood," Herry said. "This is the way to Hooper's Store. And this is the way we go to visit our friends Ernie and Bert."

Herry's new shoes did not feel so stiff as he walked up and down Sesame Street. Herry showed them Big Bird's nest and Oscar's can, and he was careful to walk around a puddle.

"You must stay away from puddles," Herry said to his sneakers. "And you must stay away from mud. Mud is not good for new shoes."

Finally, he showed his new shoes to Big Bird.

"This is the last thing I am going to show you today," Herry said, "but it is a very important thing. This is the way home."

When Herry reached his house, his mother was waiting for him. "How do you like your new shoes, my Herry Monster?" she asked.

Herry looked down at his new white sneakers with the red stripes. They weren't as white or as new-looking as when he had walked out of the shoe store.

"I think we are going to have a good time together," he said, "and we are going to be very good friends."

ONE WET MONSTER

The sun was shining, and the clouds in the sky were white and fluffy and friendly, when Grover went to the park. He did not think about taking a coat or a hat or a pair of boots. Who would need those things on a sunshiny day like today?

All afternoon Grover played with his friends in the park. He slid down the slide, and swung on the swings, and climbed on the jungle gym. He was having such a good time that he did not notice that the sky was slowly turning gray and the clouds did not look so friendly anymore. Then the wind began to blow and there was a rumble of thunder in the distance.

Everyone else hurried home, but Grover wanted to stay a few more minutes.

"I, Grover, am almost done. Certainly the rain will wait until I have finished building this beautiful castle."

But the rain did not wait. Big drops began to fall, hard and fast. "Oh, my goodness," said Grover as the raindrops splattered on his nose and fur and into the moat of his sand castle. "I had better hurry home as fast as I can. My fur is getting wet!"

Sometimes it is nice to be outside when it rains. It is nice to feel the gentle spring rain with its soft, sprinkling mist, which can make rainbows appear. It is nice to feel a summer rain as it cools the sidewalks and washes the dust from the leaves.

But this was not one of those kinds of rain. This was a *storm*. The rain was cold, and it came down in hard, driving sheets that made it hard for Grover to see what was in front of him. It was not the kind of rain a monster likes to be outside in.

Grover's mommy saw that it had started to rain. She put on her raincoat, got her umbrella, and headed toward the park to find Grover. But Grover had decided to take a different way home. So while his mommy was walking on the sidewalk to the park, Grover was running through backyards toward home.

Grover ran as fast as his monster legs could go. The rain blew in his face and soaked his fur.

"When I get to the mailbox," panted Grover, "I will have only twenty-five more steps to go. Then I will run around the corner and I will be able to see my house."

Grover tried not to think about how cold and wet he felt. He tried to think about warm, snuggly things.

"My blankie," said Grover. "I will think about my blankie and my warm, dry house. I will think about my mommy giving me a hug."

At last Grover passed the mailbox, turned the corner, and saw his house. He could see the light on, and he could see his mommy waiting for him at the door. "I came to look for you," she said, "but I could not find you."

"I took the back way home," said Grover as he shivered and dripped in the front hall.

His mommy quickly wrapped a big fluffy towel around him.
Then she filled the tub with warm water and added some
bubble bath. Grover climbed into the tub, and it made him
feel warm and tingly all over.

When he had finished his bath and he was warm and dry, Grover said, "Mommy, I was scared in that storm."

"And I was worried," said Grover's mommy, and she gave him the biggest hug a mommy monster can give her little monster. Then they sat together drinking hot chocolate and listening to the rain.

IS IT TIME FOR BED YET?

When Elmo finished his dinner, the first thing he said was, "Is it time for bed yet?"

"Why, Elmo?" asked Elmo's daddy. "Why do you want to go to bed so early? Usually you want to stay up as late as you can. Usually you find reasons not to go to bed."

"Not tonight," said Elmo. "Tonight I want to hurry up and go to sleep so that tomorrow will be here sooner. Tomorrow is the day that Grandpa is going to take me fishing."

"That is true," said Elmo's daddy. "But it seems very early to go to bed unless you are tired. Are you tired, Elmo?"

"No," said Elmo, "but Grandpa said I have to get up very early in the morning. I will make myself tired." So Elmo did twenty jumping jacks, and he touched his toes thirty times.

"Do you think I am tired yet?" Elmo asked his daddy.

"I don't know," he said. "Only you know if you're tired, Elmo."

"Maybe I could have my bath now," said Elmo. "Sometimes a bath makes me sleepy."

"All right," said Elmo's daddy, and he filled the tub with warm water. Elmo's daddy washed the fur on Elmo's back and head and behind his ears while Elmo splashed and played with his tugboat and his monster bath sponge.

When Elmo was all dry, his daddy helped him put on his pajamas.

"Now do I look tired?" Elmo asked.

"You look like a little monster who's ready for bed," said Elmo's daddy.

As Elmo climbed into bed he said, "I have a wonderful idea. I will eat breakfast now, and then get dressed in my going-fishing clothes and sleep in them. Then when Grandpa comes to get me in the morning, I will be all ready to go!"

Elmo's daddy laughed. "No, Elmo," he said, "that is not a wonderful idea. If you eat breakfast now, you will be hungry again in the morning. And you would be very uncomfortable sleeping in your jeans and shirt and rubber boots."

"Oh," said Elmo sadly.

Elmo's daddy tucked Elmo in and said, "Lie there quietly and listen while I tell you a story about the time my grandpa took me fishing when I was a little monster."

So Elmo's daddy told him how he and his grandpa had rowed a little boat on a beautiful silent lake. He told him about hearing birds singing in the early morning, and about seeing silver-colored fish jumping and splashing in the water.

As Daddy told the story the sun sank slowly and long evening shadows stretched across the room. Elmo closed his eyes. Soon he was asleep and dreaming about silver-colored fish jumping and splashing in the water on a beautiful silent lake.

SESAME STREET

When Oscar Was a Little Grouch
and Other Goodnight Stories

By Liza Alexander
Illustrated by Tom Brannon

WHEN OSCAR
WAS A LITTLE GROUCH

One day Oscar was grouch-sitting for his niece Filthomena. She was just a little slip of a grouch, no bigger than a wastepaper basket. Today Filthie was giggling and smiling and chatting. "This is terrible!" thought Oscar. "She's too perky! What would her mother say? I've got to do something to make her grouchy, and quick!"

Oscar disappeared down into his can and came back up with a pair of cymbals. *Clang! Clang! Clang!* He crashed them loudly in Filthie's ear. "Whaaaaaa!" yelled the little Grouch. "What noisy cymbals, Uncle Oscar! Where did you get them?"

"Well, little Filthie," said Oscar, "when I was your age, my mother used to say, 'Sleep grumpy, little grouch!' Then she'd play a grouch lullaby on these cymbals. They make a nice soothing racket, don't they?"

"They sure do," said Filthie. "Uncle Oscar, what was it like when you were little?"

"Funny that you should ask!" said Oscar. "I was just going through a few things I've saved from when I was an itty-bitty grouch."

Oscar ducked down into his can once again and popped back up with a chipped spoon and a battered bowl. "My mother fed me my first grouch food with this bowl and spoon. She'd say, 'Eat! It'll make you big and grouchy!'"

"Tell me more, Uncle Oscar, tell me more!" said Filthie.

"Let's see!" Oscar brought out a tiny metal trash can from his own bigger can. "This was my first real trash can. I wore it to kindergrouchen. See how battered and smashed it is! Heh, heh!"

"That can's really awful," said Filthomena. "I wish I had one just like it!"

Bang! Crash! Clank! Oscar rummaged around in his can and pulled out a bashed-up plastic flamingo and a dented toaster. "I got this junk on my very first trip to the dump," he said. "I remember it well. Uncle Oswaldo let me ride in the back of his garbage truck. It was pouring rain, and mud spattered up all over me. It was wonderful!"

"Uncle Oscar, Uncle Oscar! Will you take me to the dump sometime?" asked Filthomena.

"You bet, Filthie," said Oscar. "Anytime!"

Filthomena was so excited that she pouted furiously. She began to fuss and fret and yell. Uncle Oscar joined right in, and they had a high old grumpy time.

Filthie had really worked herself up into a fantastic fit when her mother came stomping around the corner. She gathered her little grouch up in her arms and gave her a big kiss. "Darling!" said Filthomena's mother. "Uncle Oscar must be a great grouch-sitter. I've never seen you in such a great grumpy mood. How did you do it, Oscar?"

"Shucks," said Oscar, "it was nothing!"

TINA TWIDDLEBUG'S
BIG ADVENTURE

One day Thaddeus Twiddlebug, mayor of Twiddlebug Town, said, "It is time that we build a playground for our little Twiddlebugs.

Everybody agreed, and since Twiddlebugs don't like to waste time, they got right to work. Tilly and Titus Twiddlebug used two safety pins and a toothpick to build a frame for a swing set. Then they hung buttons from string to make swings. Tessy Twiddlebug filled a matchbox with sand to make a sandbox, and Toby Twiddlebug stuck a ruler on a thimble for a seesaw.

"Marvelous, marvelous, marvelous!" said the mayor. "This playground is almost complete!"

"Just a minute!" said Tina Twiddlebug. "My Timmy loves to scramble and climb! We must have a jungle gym for our little Twiddlebugs!" Everybody agreed, but nobody could think of what would make a good jungle gym.

Tina took a deep breath and spoke up once again. "I will fly out into the big wide world and find a jungle gym for my Timmy and all the other little Twiddlebugs of our town!"

There was a hush in the crowd as all twiddling stopped. Very few Twiddlebugs had ever ventured out into the big wide world. But Mayor Thaddeus Twiddlebug was all for it. He said, "Here, here!" and clapped Tina on the back.

All the other Twiddlebugs hugged her and wished her good luck. Brave Tina gave her Timmy a big kiss and took off on her tiny Twiddlebug wings into the big wide world.

To Twiddlebugs the big wide world is any place beyond Twiddlebug Town, which is in Elmo's windowbox. And the first place next to Elmo's windowbox is Elmo's bedroom. So when Tina twiddled in through the window, Elmo was sitting on the floor playing a game of jacks.

Elmo was concentrating on his game and didn't notice Tina. And that was a good thing, because even though Elmo is a friendly little monster, Elmo seemed very big and scary to Tina. Ever so quietly Tina began to look for a jungle gym. She twiddled softly around the room.

"Elmo's checkers and his tiddlywinks would make good tables, but not good jungle gyms. His comb would make a fine fence and his dice would make nice chairs. But none of these things would be much fun to climb on. What am I to do?" wondered Tina.

Just then Elmo gave his jacks an extra big toss and one jack skittered all the way across the floor. Elmo got up and looked for it, but he couldn't find that jack anywhere. "Oh, well!" he said. "I've got plenty more jacks." The fuzzy red monster went back to his game.

But Tina, with her sharp Twiddlebug eyes, knew just where that jack had gone. She was still a little bit frightened, but when Tina Twiddlebug makes up her mind, there's no stopping her!

Tina twiddled right down behind the dresser and snatched the jack up. "It's perfect!" she thought. Off she flew, up from behind the bureau and out Elmo's window, just as fast as her tiny Twiddlebug wings could carry her.

Back in Elmo's windowbox, snug in their town, all the other Twiddlebugs waited with their fingers crossed for Tina to come back. When she did, with the jungle jack, all the Twiddlebugs sang and twiddled for joy!

"Tina," said Mayor Thaddeus Twiddlebug, "you make us proud to be Twiddlebugs!" He named her a hero and hung a bright, shiny medal around her neck.

Elmo has never figured out where that jack went, but you can be sure that to this day, thanks to Tina Twiddlebug (and Elmo), the children of Twiddlebug Town scramble and climb to their hearts' content on their very own jungle jack in their very own playground.

GOODNIGHT, BERT!

"Ooohwee!" sighed Bert. "Am I tuckered out! This old bed of mine is looking mighty inviting." Bert stretched and yawned sleepily. "Yessiree, I sure am looking forward to a little shut-eye."

"Yeah, Bert," said Ernie dreamily. "Uh, Bert? What if your pillow were really a nice fluffy cloud that you could float away on when you dream?"

"Neat idea," said Bert. "Goodnight now, Ernie."

"Just imagine," said Ernie. "You'd sail way up high in the sky. Fields would unfold beneath you like a patchwork quilt. Towns below would be tiny. Wouldn't that be something, old buddy?"

"Yes, it would be something, but if you don't mind, Ernie, I'd like to go to sleep now." Bert turned over on his side with his back to Ernie. He tugged his covers more tightly around him.

"What if your knees were mountains? Did you ever think of that, Bert?" asked Ernie.

"No, Ernie," answered Bert. "I never thought of that. Not once."

Ernie bent his knees under the covers. "Look, Bert!" said Ernie. He let his fingers do the walking up over his knees. "Bo-dee-oh-doh! My fingers are hiking up the mountains. What an excellent view! Hee, hee, hee!"

Bert didn't laugh at all. "Okay, Ernie," he said. "Very funny. Could we please get a little sleep now?"

"Anything you say, Bert. But wouldn't it be incredible if there were a huge earthquake?" Ernie shook his knees so it looked like the mountains were trembling. "Rumble, rumble," he said. *"Boom! Bang! Thunder! Lightning!* Oh, no! The mountains are tumbling down. There they go, Bert. Watch, Bert!"

Ernie knocked his knees together and the blankets rippled over them. "Geronimo!" yelled Ernie as his fingers jumped off the crumbling mountains.

"Ernieeee!" groaned Bert.

"Luckily," said Ernie, "there is no earthquake and there are no mountains, just my good old tired knees! Yep, Bert, it sure is nice to get into bed after a long day. Good night, old buddy. Sleep tight!" Ernie yawned and snuggled down under his covers. Soon he was snoring soundly.

Bert couldn't sleep. He sat up and peeked over at Ernie to make sure his friend was truly asleep. Then Bert bent his knees like Ernie so they looked like mountains. Bert walked his fingers up the mountains. At the top of the mountains his fingers paused. "Good night, knees!" said Bert. Then he walked his fingers step-by-step down the mountain and over the covers. Bert began to relax. He hummed, "Bo-dee-oh-doh!" His pillow felt soft as a cloud. "Good night, pillow!" whispered Bert. Then he drifted off into a deep, sweet sleep.